My Writer

by

Jilly Henderson-Long

ISBN: 978-1-326-00632-7

PublishNation, London
www.publishnation.co.uk

FOR ANDREW, OLIVIA, ISAAC,
SOPHIE, HARRY AND JACK
WITH LOVE XX

VICKY WRITES

Dear Dickie Doyle.
Thank you for writing the Wizardatron
Books. They are brilliant! I love reading
about his magic adventures. I wonder if
he will ever ever get back. Please keep on
writing them. When is the next one out?
I am truly your biggest fan.
Vicky Price
Age 8 ½

1 - My Brother

"It must be sooo cool to have a famous brother, Vicky!" This has been said to me so many times now that I don't even hear it anymore. There's usually a bunch of us just standing around, talking about stuff - like homework, or school or the weekend, then someone says "Vicky. I said it must be sooo cool to have a famous brother ..." and I look at them as if they're talking a foreign language. "Your brother," they'll say. "Daniel." As if I don't know my own brother. Mind you it sometimes feels like I don't know him. Or Mum and Dad. Anyway, I look at them and they talk to me like I'm a complete nut-job and say, "So what's it like?" "What's what like?" I ask. I get the big drama queen sigh and rolled eyes before they say, slowly, "What's it like having a famous brother?"

Sometimes, I say something like, "It's great! Did you see him on 'Eastenders' last week?" or "It *is* cool. He's auditioning for 'Oliver'..." Anything to make them jealous even though I know that's not very nice. But mostly I just say "It's gross." and leave it at that. They try to get me talking but I won't. It's all right for them. Sometimes they don't realise just how bored I get with the whole famous-brother thing. Especially when they start fluttering their eyelashes and begging for his autograph. "Oh, please, Vick. Please get it for me. He's sooo cute!" Cute! My brother? He might look cute on television but when he *is* home (which isn't that often), he's just like all older brothers. He sulks. He picks his nose. He teases me or gets into a strop. I still love him to bits though. Only don't tell him I said so or it'll be all over Facebook before you know it.

It's kind of funny because I don't think of him as being a famous actor - he's just Daniel. He's two years older than me and he's been acting and stuff since he was three so all I've ever known of Daniel is seeing him on TV. To be honest I do get sick of it because he gets all the attention and I don't think that's fair. Ever since he started acting he's hardly been home at all so we've never really done what brothers and sisters usually do. We've never been swimming together or gone riding our bikes or played each other on Playstation. Right now for instance, he's in America filming a Dickie Doyle book - 'Wizardatron 1 - Lost In the Void'. I mean Dickie Doyle! He's my most favourite writer ever ever *ever*. And Daniel's in the film!

Another thing is that I don't usually tell people about Dan. Sometimes, someone tells a new kid at school and the new kid comes up to me and says something like "Is it true you're Daniel Price's sister?" I usually say "No. But it's true he's my brother." Then the whole it-must-be-so-cool-to-have-a-famous-brother thing starts again. It's freaky and just about sends me mad.

I do sometimes get to talk to him though and we send each other emails or have a quick chat on the phone. Funnily enough, we had a web-cam chat yesterday.

"So - how's everything?" he asked.

"All right," I told him.

"Nan okay?"

"She's great. She's booked a table for us at Pizza Parlour for my birthday next week and I can't wait. When do you and Mum get home?"

"Should be Monday," Dan answered. "Do you want anything special for your birthday, Vick?"

"Something American," I answered.

"Like what?" he said.

3

"I don't know. Surprise me."

"I'll see what's about," Daniel said. "Gotta go. See you Monday." Then he'd gone. That's how most of our chats are these days. My nana says they're 'short and to the point'. I call them a waste of time because we never have long enough to really talk about anything. I wanted to ask him what it's like doing the Wizardatron film and whether he's met Dickie Doyle yet. But I didn't have the chance. I know there's a couple of other famous British actors in it. One of them is Simon Pegg - have you heard of him?

"Was that Dan?" asked my nana walking into my room.

"Yep. He sends his love," I told her. "Him and Mum'll be back Monday. He said he'd bring me something American for my birthday."

"Aren't you the lucky one," said Nana, kissing my head. "Now get your jammies on. It's bed time."

A bit later, after she'd gone back downstairs, I laid in bed trying to imagine what it feels like to be in a Dickie Doyle film but all I could think of was Daniel's face! He is a good actor I suppose. He knows how to pretend to cry and get real tears and everything.

"Per-lease get me his autograph, Vick," said one of the stupid girls from school in my head. "He's sooo cute!" And suddenly, I fell asleep.

2 - My Dad and Mum

We're a bit of a funny family really. My dad works with precious stones and travels all over the world. Right now, he's in Egypt doing something about a blood diamond whatever that is. He's always off on business and he always looks dead smart in his suits and really handsome. No wonder Mum fancied him. He looks like *he* should be a film star and he's good fun to have around. When he *is* around that is - which isn't very often really. He loves sneaking into Burger King. I say 'sneaking' because he says that, as a successful businessman, he's only expected to be seen eating at really posh places where a bowl of soup cost fifty quid or something like that.

When he was a kid, my dad used to sing in a band. He still tells stories about girls throwing their knickers at him when he sang. How totally gross is that? How can that be something to boast about? Sounds sick to me but he says it's really true.

Because he works so hard and travels so much he gets paid loads and loads of money and every time he goes away, he sends me some. I usually go out and buy books with it because I think books are the best thing in the world. Sometimes I buy a pen and a nice notebook because I want to be a famous writer one day, like Dickie Doyle.

My dad's name is Harrison. I know someone whose surname is Harrison so I think it's a bit weird to have it as a first name. He loves Manchester United, my dad. And loads of different kinds of music and he likes taking pictures of all the countries he goes to. We have got albums full of them. I think it's my dad I miss the most, really, even though we don't do any of the things other kids do with their dads - and I can't remember the last time we all went on holiday together.

My mum's different as well. Her name is Penelope and she goes everywhere with Daniel as his chaperone, so I hardly ever see her either. She's a lot younger than my dad and really pretty and she always looks lovely, whatever she's wearing. I know she loves me a lot but we've never been shopping together or had our nails done like other girls do with their mums.

My mum always wanted to be a dancer. When she was my age, she did lots of it and she was always appearing in shows. She even won a scholarship to some famous dance school in London. But when she was thirteen she was run over by a car and both her legs were broken in lots of places. And although she was really brave and learned to walk quicker than any of the doctors thought she would, she never became a famous dancer or went to the famous school in London. My nana thinks that's why she is so proud of Daniel being an actor. Like she can live the life she wanted through him. At least that's what Nana thinks. I don't know what to think half the time.

I get really moody some days, I know that. It isn't only when the kids at school start on about my famous brother either. It's mostly when they come into school talking about what they've done with their families. Like they'll say they went swimming with their dad or had a nice girly chat with their mum. A girly chat? What's one of those then? Or they'll say how their mum helped them to choose what to wear, or they helped their mum to choose to what to wear. Then they look at me and say "And what did you do at the weekend, Vicky?" Till I end up wanting to yell or scream or kick something.

Sometimes, I don't think life is fair, really. That's one of the reasons Nana suggested I start keeping a diary. This isn't exactly a diary, I know that. But it's a good way to say how I'm feeling.

Which isn't all that great right now, so I'm off. More later.

3 - My Nana

Sorry about that. Told you I get moody. When I went downstairs, Nana looked up and said "What's the matter, Popsicle?" She always calls me that and I like it. Anyway, i told her nothing was the matter but I could feel my face getting hotter and hotter. Then suddenly, I burst out crying. That just happens sometimes. I don't know why. Like the other week, it happened at school. There we all were writing our book reviews in English and it just happened. And the problem is that once I start it takes me ages to stop. It's a bit embarrassing. So that day Miss Rupert took me to see the nurse who gave me a cup of tea and just chatted away until I felt better. Then I went back to class. I didn't tell Nana because I knew she'd worry, but the school rang her so she found out anyway.

So - getting back to last night - when I started crying, Nana wrapped her arms around me and I cried all over her till her jumper was wet. Then she gave me a tissue and I wiped my eyes. After a bit she said gently "So what was all that about?"

Let me tell you a bit about my nana. Firstly, you probably think I'm too old to call her Nana. People seem to think that at my age - almost eleven - I should be more grown up and call her Nan but I've tried and I just can't. She has always been Nana to me and I know that she is my best friend in the world. The kids at school think she's pretty cool because she isn't like people usually expect Nanas to be. For a start, she always wears jeans and trainers. She doesn't knit and she moans even if she has to sew on a button. She hates baking cakes. She says "Why bake them when you can pop down the baker's and buy them?" She doesn't mind doing a bit of gardening or decorating and she likes watching football and rugby. And the American wrestlers when she shouts at the screen and yells "Grab him! Bring him down! Oh no - a pile-driver!" She's got long curly brown hair with grey streaks in it. She's my mum's mum and only twenty years older which makes her fifty-five.

When Daniel started acting, he was always at auditions and, because Dad was away so much and Mum was chaperoning Daniel, that only left Nana to look after me. Don't forget, I was only two when it all started so, for almost nine years now, I have been living with my nana.

At first, Mum's younger brother was there too, my Uncle Pete - but he moved to Scotland so we hardly ever see him these days. He's a wildlife photographer and he lives in an Artist's House near a tiny town in the mountains called Braemar and that's a good place for him with all the wildlife up there. Once Uncle Pete moved out that only left me and Nana so that was that.

My nana's a poet. She writes loads of it and she's had loads published too. I don't read them though because I like adventure stories like Dickie Doyle writes. And they're the sort of stories I want to write one day, too.

Anyway, Nana asked me why I got upset and I couldn't tell her because she must get sick of me moaning about missing everyone, so I just said I didn't know. Then she asked me if everything's all right at school and I told her school's the same as usual. I think she could tell I didn't want to talk about it because she gave me another hug and then said why don't we watch a DVD and have a chocolate shake, so that's what we did. And - because she likes everything perfect, we closed all the curtains

9

and turned all the lights off and turned the volume up until it sounded like we were in a cinema. We watched a film about Beatrix Potter which is one of our favourites - especially the bit when Beatrix Potter is handed her first published book. That'll be me, one day, you just watch.

After the DVD, we cleared up together, then I had a shower and when my hair was dry, I went to bed. Nana came up after a while to make sure I wasn't crying again (she didn't say that was why she'd come up, but I know it was) and she sat on the bed beside me.

"So what are you reading now?" she asked. Of course it was one of my Dickie Doyle books.

"Look at this," she said, handing me a sheet of newspaper. "Dickie Doyle's going to do a tour…"

"Really?" I gasped and snatched the paper and read it. The headline was 'ENIGMA DICKIE DOYLE _WILL_ TOUR' and I'll copy out the report for you. It went - *Kid's favourite Dickie Doyle will do a promotional tour to coincide with the launch of the new Wizardatron book 'The Purple Lightning' sources have revealed. The camera-shy writer has always fiercely protected his privacy and is believed to have been tempted into the limelight by his ever-growing army of Wizardatron fans. The new book is due out on 16th July but no venue had yet been announced.*

I can't believe it! *Dickie Doyle is going to tour*!!!

4 - My Dickie Doyle

So here's where I tell you about my most favourite writer ever ever *ever.* He's had ten books published and two of those are the first two Wizardatron ones which are the best of all. Wizardatron books are a mixture of adventure and what Nana calls Fantasy Sci-Fi. That means they're all about aliens and black holes and time warps. Dickie Doyle's wizard is from the future and the books are about him trying to get back. It sounds kind of stupid when I say it like that but if you've ever read any, you'll know what I mean.

I'm not sure when I first started reading Dickie Doyle books. In fact, I can't remember a time I couldn't read. It's like I've been able to read ever since I was born which I know isn't possible, it's just how it feels to me. I've always loved books and one day, I read a Dickie Doyle book. Then I read another one. After that I just couldn't stop. I've read every single one of them at least five times and that's totally true. A couple of months ago, Nana bought me a scrap book and I have filled it up with Dickie Doyle stuff. Not sure if that makes me some kind of saddo or what, but I do like looking through it.

Dickie Doyle is really famous but nobody knows what he looks like because he hates having his photo taken. He says his writing speaks for him so he doesn't need to do anything else. Which is why I was so surprised to find out he's going to do a tour. The papers say he is married with two kids and used to be a teacher. How cool must that be - to have someone like Dickie Doyle for your dad? How do the kids keep it so quiet? If he was my dad I'd have to tell everyone, I just wouldn't be able to help it because I'd be so proud. When I'm a writer like him I'll make sure everyone knows. It would be nice to be more famous than Daniel for five minutes and one day I will be.

I still can't believe it about the tour. Dickie Doyle *never* does book tours, everyone knows that. Maybe they're going to build it up a lot - just so we'll all go crazy waiting. I know I will.

After Nana brought up some sticky tape, I put that report into my Dickie Doyle scrap book but I felt too excited to sleep and I kept getting it out to read. When I did get to sleep all I dreamt about was how I'd meet Dickie Doyle one day. And that's quite hard when you don't know what someone looks like. So maybe I am a bit of a saddo. Even if I *have* got a famous brother!

5 - My Library

Went to the library today. I really love it there. It's magic, it really is. I don't mean rabbits-coming-out-of-hats magic - I mean talking-to-me magic. Every time I go to that library, I hear all this whispering - not scary whispering - it's more like every book in the place is inviting me to read it; as if all the characters in all the books are saying "Choose me, today, Vicky." I asked Nana about it, one day. She says it happens to her as well and is a special gift that only a few people have got so it isn't all that weird. I still haven't told anyone else though. It's our secret - mine, Nana's and the library's. You should try listening for it one day, you never know.

Our library is in a big old fashioned house on the other side of the park. The kids' section is upstairs and the adults' section is downstairs. There's also a computer room downstairs but I only ever go to the kids' section because that's where I feel the magic is strongest. I have been going there ever since I was really tiny. My nana used to take me to story time there. The librarians are brilliant at reading the stories - they do all the voices and everything.

Now I've grown up a bit I go on my own like that kid Matilda in the Roald Dahl book *and* I've read quite a few of the books on her list as well. If she was real I am almost sure she'd feel the magic, too. The kids' section at our library has got picture books one end, reference books the other end and masses of fiction in the middle. I usually go straight to the 'D' section just so I can see all the Dickie Doyle books lined up on the shelf. There's usually a lot of kids reading his stuff. I always just grab one then plop onto one of the big cushions they've got all over the place and just read and read and read. The thing is that once I start reading, I just never want to stop and I end up rushing to get home on time. In fact, one time, my nana even rang the library to ask if they'd seen me because it was almost six o'clock and I hadn't got home from school yet. Bev - who's my favourite librarian - came over and tapped me on the shoulder.

"You Nan's just rung," she said. "And we're closing any minute." Closing! But they never shut till six. I looked at the clock. It was almost six. I couldn't believe it. The last time I'd looked at the clock it was only just after four. I'd been lost in Wizardatron 1 for two hours! Nana gave me a right telling off that day I can tell you. I felt really bad because I could see she'd been worried sick. I kept saying sorry and after a bit she gave me a cuddle and said sorry for yelling at me and I promised her I'd always get in by five from then on and I always do.

Anyway there was loads of excitement at the library today because of the Dickie Doyle tour. Everyone was trying to guess what Dickie Doyle looks like. And they wanted to know if he'll say hello and *then* sign the book or will he just sign it and not say a word. I really didn't mean to listen but I couldn't help it. One kid said "I bet he's really ugly and that's why they've hidden him away for so long." Another kid said "Maybe he looks like one of his monsters." "He can't look like one of his monsters because they're made up and there's no such thing as real monsters," argued the first kid. "I didn't say he *is* a monster," said the second kid. "I only said maybe he *looks* like one." "Don't be an idiot all your life," said the first kid. "He's probably just a bit shy." "How would you know?" asked the second kid. "Is he your *boyfriend*?" They got into quite a big argument till Bev came over and shushed them. After they'd shushed, she said to me,

"What do you think, Vicky? I know you're a big fan of his."

"I think it's great," I said. "I hope he comes round here. I'd love to meet him, I really would."

"If I was you," Bev said, "I'd keep an eye on the internet so you can find out the dates and get to one of the signings." She went off to stamp some books and I got back to reading. A while later, I heard someone say,

"… um … uh … writer …" I looked up pretty quickly and saw this odd looking man talking to Bev. I'm not sure why he caught my eye. Lots of people talk to Bev because there's nothing she doesn't know about books, but she wasn't directing him anywhere and he kept moving his feet as if the floor was too hot for him to stand on. I heard her say "Call that number …" He said "… um … right …" He put a slip of paper into his pocket and that was when he saw me looking at him. But I couldn't help it because he was so weird-looking. Not ugly or scary - just weird. He had long hair right past his shoulders and round glasses. He was wearing a stripy jumper that looked about ten sizes too big for him and - and here's the really weird bit - *odd trainers*.

As soon as he saw me looking at him he turned away but even then he didn't actually go anywhere.

"Was there anything else, Mr Spoon?" Bev asked.

"Um … no …" he said and as he walked through the door, it bounced back and almost hit his head. I went over to Bev.

"Is he a writer?" I asked.

"So he says," Bev answered. "His name's …" She looked at the business card he'd handed her. "Jimmy Spoon." We both laughed at that. It sounded such an odd name and Terry - who's another librarian came over and told *us* to be quiet.

I looked at the clock and saw it was almost five so I came home. After dinner I came up to my room and turned on the laptop and put "Jimmy Spoon" into Google - but nothing came up about him. Just then, Nana walked in.

"Shall we go shopping tomorrow?" she asked. I thought she meant food shopping which I hate so I moaned out loud. "Not food shopping," Nana laughed. Then she peered over my shoulder.

"Jimmy Spoon?" she said sounding really surprised. I nodded.

"He was at the library today," I told her. "He told Bev he's a writer, but I've never heard of him and there's nothing on the internet about him."

"He *is* a writer," said Nana. "He was a student of mine when I ran those Creative Writing classes. But that was ten years ago. Last time I heard from him he was working in Jersey. Well, well. Fancy that. So you up for some shopping tomorrow then?"

"What are we buying?" I asked.

"A new dress for you," said Nana. "Because after all, a certain young lady turns eleven next week, doesn't she?"

6 - My Shopping Trip

Spent all day today in town with Nana. There's nothing she likes more than what she calls 'a bit of retail therapy'. We started off like we always do at Caffe Nero where I had hot chocolate with sprinkles and she had a cappuccino and we shared a chocolate muffin. After that, we started looking for the new dress and we tried just about every place you can think of. You see, I don't really like dresses - I think they're for babies. I prefer jeans or leggings but Nana kept on and on and on about how nice it would be if I had a nice new dress to wear at my birthday meal and I could see she'd made up her mind so that was that. In the end I chose a dark blue one. It's quite straight and loose so we got a red belt and a red headband to go with it and when you put it all together it doesn't look half bad. Nana said the red headband would really set off my dark brown hair and she seemed happy enough.

After the clothes shopping, we went to Macdonalds for lunch. Then I begged Nana to come to Benjy's Books with me because it really is my favourite book shop. There was loads of posters up for the book tour. It's clever how they've done it. There's a photo of a book case stuffed with Dickie Doyle books and in front of that is a man's shadow with the words "Will Dickie Doyle Stop Here?" on it. At the bottom it says "Watch This Space For Details". Nana says it's all a 'load of hype and hullabaloo'. She thinks that the publishers are keeping everyone waiting on purpose, just to keep everyone's interest. If that's true, I think it's a good way to do it because Benjy's was packed today.

In Benjy's, I left Nana having a chat with Benjy as I walked around. Benjy is another of Nana's old students and is actually a lady with lovely golden brown skin, who writes yucky love stories. Nana seems to have a lot of old students. Anyway, I heard her say to Benjy,

"My Popsicle only bumped into Jimmy Spoon yesterday."

"Jimmy Spoon!" said Benjy. "I can't believe it. I wonder what he's been up to all this time then?"

"No idea," said Nana. "She didn't talk to him but she heard him talking to Bev. Apparently he's still writing."

"Ah - Bev - the librarian," said Benjy. "Didn't know who you meant at first. Do you think he's still writing those horror stories?"

"Possibly," said Nana. "He always fancied himself as the next Stephen King." Stephen who? "So I said to Popsicle to tell him I said hi next time."

"Do you ever hear from anyone else Babs?" asked Benjy (I always forget her name's Babs - or Barbara - she's just Nana to me).

"Only you," Nana grinned.

"Do you ever think about running those courses again?" Benjy wanted to know.

"At my age?" said Nana. "You *are* joking. I like being at home in the evenings nowadays. Haven't got the energy to go traipsing off to night classes anymore."

By now I'd picked a couple of books out and I asked if I could have them. One was "Heidi" and the other was "Just William". Nana gave me a funny look but she bought them for me anyway and Benjy put them into one of her brown recycled Benjy's Books bags as Nana paid for them. Aren't I lucky to have a nana like her?

By the time we got home, it was raining so we rushed out to the garden to get the washing in, then I started reading "Heidi" while Nana cooked bolognaise for dinner. As we were eating, I said,

"Why is Benjy called Benjy, Nana?"

"Because," said Nana, "that's her name."

"But it's a boy's name," I said.

"Well her parents obviously didn't think so," said Nana. "Now stop talking and eat up."

We were half way through dinner when the phone rang. It was my dad. He can't get back for my birthday next week.

"Why not?" I asked.

"Because, darling, I have got a very important meeting in Dubai and I can't miss it. I'm so sorry, baby."

"Don't call me baby!" I screamed at him. "You promised me!"

"I know, Vicky, and I'm sorry. I'll get back as soon as I can, okay."

"It'll be too late!" I screeched. "I'm only going to be eleven once aren't I!" I was crying my eyes out. Nana took the phone and put her arm round my shoulders.

"Well done, Harrison," she said softly and put down the phone.

So now you know. My dad isn't going to be at Pizza Parlour next week!

7 - My Special Mission

It took me a couple of days to get over Dad's call. I was so furious that if he'd of been around I'd have thrown something at him. Something hard and heavy that would hurt. He sent me a big bunch of flowers which arrived today and had a sorry message. But I just gave them to Nana who put them in water.

When I woke up this morning, I felt a bit better. Mum and Daniel should be home tomorrow as long as the flight isn't delayed like last time when they were stuck at JFK Airport for sixteen hours. They'll be jet-lagged so I won't see them properly till Tuesday, I suppose, but at least they'll be here, unlike my dad.

At breakfast, Nana said,

"You seem a bit brighter today, Popsicle."

"Well - I suppose it isn't really Dad's fault if he's got to work, is it," I answered. She ruffled my hair.

"That's my Popsicle," she said. "Now, what shall we do today?"

Sunday's always a funny day for us. Sometimes we go to church. Other times we stay at home and 'potter about' as Nana puts it. And sometimes, we jump on a bus and see where we end up. Today was a jump-on-a-bus day and we ended up in Bromley. We don't go there that often but they've got a brilliant Waterstones there and a Steiff Bear shop. That's Nana's favourite because she collects Steiff bears. We've got cabinets full of them and she loves them to bits. We went to the Steiff shop first and Nana 'treated' herself to a chocolate brown bear called Fudge who's about sixteen centimetres long and cost about a hundred quid. Then we had lunch at Spudu-Like. My best one is the cheese and beans one but Nana likes the tuna and sweet corn one best.

In Waterstones, they had some of the Will-Dickie-Doyle-Stop-Here? posters up. I said to Nana,

"How will anyone recognise Dickie Doyle if no-one knows what he looks like?"

"I wouldn't worry too much," Nana said. "As soon as he makes his first appearance *everyone* will know what he looks like because he'll be all over the papers."

"How comes he doesn't like having his picture taken?" I asked. "After all he *is* a famous writer."

"Actually he *isn't* famous is he?" said Nana. "His *name* is famous and his books are. But Dickie Doyle himself is probably just a shy person who likes to write." This is why I love my nana so much. She's got all the answers to everything. When I was little she used to say "Nanas know everything." And she does too.

"If I ever get to be a writer, " I said, "I'll make sure everyone knows who I am."

"You mean *when* you get to be a writer," corrected Nana. "Anyway - I'm a writer and nobody knows me. There's more to being a writer than being famous, Popsicle. Besides - one famous person in the family is quite enough. I knew a poet once who wrote 'fame can be a steady flame that bids to people stay, or a cruel glare that blinds a person's sight'."

"Wow Nana!" I gasped. "That is so true." I knew exactly what she meant. Don't ask me how, I just did. Maybe having Daniel for a brother helped.

"I'll set you a challenge," said Nana. "See if you can find out anything else about Dickie Doyle - including what he looks like - and I'll make sure you get to meet him at one of the signings."

"And how am I meant to do that?" I asked. Her eyes

twinkled.

"That's the challenge," she said.

So that's what I have been trying to do all afternoon. When you google him it just brings up all the usual stuff that everyone knows about him. Plus there's loads about the book tour and the new film. I was just about to give up when I saw something that really surprised me because I didn't know about it before. Know what it is? There's a Dickie Doyle Fan Club! Can you believe that? I think it must be new because I've never heard of it before and I am his biggest fan so if anyone knew about it, it would be me. Maybe it is all part of that hullaballoo Nana mentioned? Anyway, I checked the website out and found loads of stuff on there about his books but hardly a thing about Dickie Doyle! I don't get it. There's a question and answer page and a blog where he writes about what he's been doing. But no photos of him or his family - just his dog who's called Rex. What a totally boring name! Couldn't he call it something like Wiz after the Wizardatron books? I would if I was him and I had a dog.

I decided to join the fan club. Nana said she'll pay for it with her credit card because she set me the challenge. It says new members will receive a welcome pack with a newsletter, a badge, a Dickie Doyle notebook and pen and - *his autograph*! That's it then. What's he going to sign? A bus ticket? A blank sheet of paper? No - it will just *have* to be a photograph. What else is there?

I filled out the online form so all I can do now is wait. I hope the welcome pack arrives before he starts the tour. I want to go up to him and shake his hand and say "Hello Mister Doyle. Thank you for the signed photograph." He'll be surprised someone's actually recognised him, won't he?

8 - My Bad Head Day

Woke up yesterday feeling terrible. I think it was because I'd been crying most of the night. I'll tell you why in a bit. Right now I want to think about anything else I can, so in a second, I'll tell you a bit more about Jimmy Spoon.

This morning, when Nana said "No school for you today," I just went straight back to bed and cried some more. Nana's at her wit's end. I know because I heard her say so. She actually used those words "I'm really at my wit's end!"

After a bit, she came back up to see me. She sat on the bed beside me and wiped my face with a cold flannel because, she said, it was all swollen and blotchy - especially my eyes. The cold flannel was really soothing and made me feel a bit better straight away.

"Want to talk about it?" she asked. I rolled over on my side and didn't answer because talking about it was the last thing in the world I wanted. She grasped my shoulder and turned me back to face her.

"Okay, we won't," she said. "Not till you're ready." She dabbed at my eyes again and tried to smile. It didn't work very well because her eyes were much too shiny.

"So," she said instead. "What would you like to do instead of school?" I shrugged and her pretend smile faded away.

"Now listen, Vicky," she said. "I know you're cross and disappointed and that's perfectly okay. But you can't sit up here all day feeling sorry for yourself. You're getting a whole day off school. You should do something nice to cheer yourself up."

"I don't want to do anything," I said. It came out all sulky but I couldn't help it.

"Well then the whole day will be wasted," she said. "Why don't you try to write a story? You keep saying you're going to be a writer."

"Well I don't want to be one today," I grouched.

"Why not?" Nana asked.

"I just don't." I folded my arms and stared at her. I knew it wasn't fair to be cross with Nana but I was cross with everyone - myself most of all. Nana sighed but then she said,

"I'll tell you what. I am going to have a shower. You can fume in here for as long as you like. But I'd like you to calm down and have a proper answer to that question when I come back."

"What question?" I asked.

"About what you'd like to do today," said Nana.

"I told you!" I screamed at her. "I don't want to do anything."

"You think about it," she said. She walked off to have her shower and I looked around my room. Everything was there in its place - my bean bag piled high with teddies, my desk, laptop, CD player, DVD player, all my special post cards and pictures. It all *looked* right, but none of it *felt* right. So I did what I always do. I started reading. Not Dickie Doyle this time - I didn't even want to *think* about Wizardatron - but 'Heidi', which is about as far away as you can get. By the time, Nana came back in all fresh and smelling flowery like outdoors, I'd made up my mind.

"So," she said. "Have you decided?"

"Yes," I said. "I want to go to the library."

"That's my good girl," Nana said. "Why don't you go and have a shower yourself, get dressed and, after some breakfast, we'll head off to the library."

My nana likes a plan. She loves being organised. So I actually did what she said. I even used some of her flowery shower stuff. After I was dressed and we were munching toast in the kitchen, I said,

"Nana suppose someone from school sees me at the library instead of at school? What will you say?"

"That you weren't well enough for school but chose to go to the library in order to use your day off constructively," she answered.

"But I'm not really ill am I ?" I said. She looked at me.

"Do you *want* to go to school?" she asked. I thought about that for a minute. I couldn't stand the thought of the so-cool-to-have-a-famous-brother gang in my face all day, so I shook my head.

"No," I said. "Not today."

"It'll be okay, Vicky," Nana said. "Stop being such a worry-wart." That's one of her sayings. Believe me, she's got loads.

So that's what we did. We went to the library, Nana and me. She came up to the kid's section with me but once she could see I was okay, she went off to 'do some research' downstairs and said that we'd go out for some lunch later.

I was on my belly on a cushion when I looked up and spotted Jimmy Spoon. He was sitting at the round wooden table - the one that's kid-sized - on a kid sized chair. His legs looked really long and gangly and his knees were almost round his ears. He was hunched over, scribbling something. I know it's rude to stare but I couldn't help it. Where the sun was shining through the window, his long curly hair looked almost like it was glowing. And he was wearing odd trainers. Again.

After a bit, he looked up at me and, straight away, his face went really red - and he looked away again. I closed my book, got up and went over to him. He knew I was there but he pretended he didn't. He just kept scribbling away. I said,

"You're Jimmy Spoon." He looked up quickly - and sent his notebook and pen flying across the floor. He said in a shaky voice,

"… um …"

"My nana knows you," I said. He leaned over to pick up his notebook and pen - and fell off of the kid-sized chair. Then, as he tried to stop himself, he knocked over the table as well.

"… Um …" he said again. He was in a right tangle and I could see him shaking all over. I stood the chair up and he stood the table up. Then I bent down and picked up his notebook and pen and held them towards him.

"What you writing then?" I asked.

"… Um .." said Jimmy Spoon again. It seemed to be the only thing he *could* say.

"My nana used to be your teacher," I said.

"Oh …" he said.

"She says you're a writer," I told him. "But I've never heard of you…"

"Who … um … who's your …Nan … um … then?" he asked. He still wouldn't look at me.

"She's downstairs," I said. "Shall I get her for you?"

"Er … um … no," said Jimmy Spoon. He took his notebook and pen and shoved them into his rucksack. "I'm … um … kind of … um … in a hurry, so …um …"

"Jimmy!" said Nana's voice. We both looked towards the door. She was coming in with an armful of books.

"Oh … er … B-babs …" said Jimmy Spoon. I looked at him amazed. They really did know each other! Nana came over, set the books on the table and looked for a second, as if she was going to hug him. But she patted his arm instead.

"So how are you?" she asked.

"Oh … um …you know … same ol' same ol'" Jimmy Spoon answered.

"My grand-daughter told me she'd seen you in here. I couldn't believe you'd resurfaced after all these years. How have you been?"

"Oh … um … this is … your …" Jimmy Spoon said. Nana put her arm round my shoulders.

"This is Vicky," she said.

"Wow … um … Vicky … you've er … grown …" Jimmy Spoon said. I looked at Nana in surprise.

"Well it *has* been ten years since I brought those first baby photos in, you know, Jimmy," said Nana. "Vicky lives with me."

"Uh … right …" said Jimmy Spoon. He still wouldn't look at me and I noticed he was edging towards the door.

"Well … um …B-babs. I've … um ..got to …um …" He pushed his glasses up his nose and nodded towards the door.

"I'll … er … see you … um …then …" he said. Nana handed him one of her business cards. She's always got a few of them on her.

"Drop me an email," she said.

"Um …" Jimmy Spoon nodded.

"You take care," said Nana.

"Right …" said Jimmy Spoon. "You … too … um … you two too …" He hurried away without looking back.

"What a weirdo," I said. "How can he be a good writer when he can hardly talk?"

"So," said Nana. "Are you all done?" I hadn't even started.

"Five more minutes," I said. Nana nodded.

"Five more minutes it is then," she said.

9 - My Birthday

Yesterday, Tuesday - I went back to school. Oh! I forgot to tell what had happened didn't I? Well, you've probably guessed it. Mum and Daniel won't be back for my birthday because Dan's been delayed in Detroit for at least a week because of filming. We got the phone call on Sunday night. When Mum told me I just felt for a second as if no-one in the world, except Nana, loves me. She took the phone off me and said,

"Penelope, you can't let Vicky down like this again, you just can't! She's been looking forward to her birthday for weeks because she thought you'd all be there. Yes. Yes I understand that but Vicky needs you too and it's not fair. I know. I know that but she puts up with a lot from you three. No, Penelope. No I am not trying to make you feel worse than you already do, but it's time she got some of your time as well. I know. Yes, I know - but it's okay for you, you're not the one who has to pick up he pieces are you? I'm really at my wit's end, Penelope. It took her two days to get over Harrison's call - and now this. She's eleven on Wednesday, Penelope. It's no use screaming down the phone at me, you're the one who won't be here for her birthday!" On and on and on until, in the end, Nana just hung up on her. No wonder I was crying nearly all night - anyone would, wouldn't they?

Anyways. I woke up this morning and it didn't feel like my birthday at all. Nana was waiting for me in the kitchen. She'd cooked my favourite breakfast - French Toast - and she'd got some of my favourite pineapple juice so we had a nice breakfast. There were a few cards by my plate. One each from Mum, Dad and Daniel and one from Uncle Pete. The biggest and best one was from Nana.

"Are we still going to Pizza Parlour tomorrow, even though, it'll only be us?" I asked her.

"Do you want to?" she asked back. I thought about it then nodded. Their garlic bread is the best in the world and their mushroom pizza is my absolute favourite.

"Then we'll still go," said Nana. "I'll just call today and ask for a smaller table." Then she told me she'd had an email from Jimmy Spoon. She showed it to me. It said -

Babs - good to bump into you.

Sorry I couldn't linger for a chat,

things to do, you know how it is.

It would be nice to catch up and

- since we're almost neighbours,

I'm sure we can sort something out

if you like. Best as ever - Jimmy Spoon.

He writes better than he talks, don't you think? I asked Nana if he'd always been a nervous wreck and she said the only time he isn't is when he's reading his work out. He writes ghost stories - or at least he used to. Oh yes - and I found out who Stephen King is as well. He's an American writer.   My nana loves him as much as I love Dickie Doyle. Soon as she told me, I remembered. She has got shelves full of his books - he's written about forty million!

Back to today then. Well, I didn't tell anyone at school it is my birthday because I haven't got any proper friends at school. That bothers Nana a lot. She's always asking why I don't have friends my own age but I don't need them. The girls are only interested in my 'famous brother' anyway and I don't trust them. There is this one girl - Jennifer Armstrong. When she first started there, she didn't know about Daniel and, to start with, we were great

29

mates. But then one weekend she came for a sleep-over - and went straight to Daniel's room so someone must of told her. She kept touching his stuff, sitting on his bed and begging to sleep there when Nana had already set a fold-away bed up for her in my room. So I never asked her over again and we've not been friends since then.

I had a pretty normal day at school and afterwards went to the library. Bev gave me a card and - even though she wasn't meant to, she gave me one of the Will-Dickie-Doyle-Stop-Here posters. It was the best present I got - apart from the chocolate brown Steiff bear Nana had told me she'd bought for herself. I was wondering why he hadn't appeared in one of the cabinets with all the others. Nana also gave me some money which she says, is from my invisible family. But I know better.

"This isn't from them, Nana, it's from you!" I said crossly. "I'm not stupid you know." She grinned and said,

"My clever Popsicle! You never miss a thing do you? Okay - I admit it. It *is* from me but they have all promised to pay me back so it *is* kind of from them." I didn't know whether to believe her or not. In the end I said, in my horrible sulky voice,

"Well that was nice of them wasn't it!"

"Now, now," said Nana. "It's not like you to be sarcastic!" Before it could turn into another row, she hugged me and we ended up laughing.

"You do know they love you, don't you, Sweetheart?" she said after a bit. I nodded. I know they do. Of course they do. I just wish they could've got back for my birthday, that's all.

Anyway while I was at the library, I went onto one of the computers to see if I could find any photos of Dickie Doyle because I haven't forgotten my challenge. He hasn't got a facebook page and the only blog I could find was on the fan club website and we don't really know, do we, that he writes it himself or, like Nana thinks - that someone else writes it for him.

After that I went up to the kid's section and I was reading 'Wind In The Willows' when a voice said,

"Er ... hi... Vicky ..." It was Jimmy Spoon! He gave me one of his funny little half smiles then handed me a blue envelope.

"B-babs ... uh ... your nan ... said it's your ... um ... b-birthday ... uh ... today so ... um ... hap ... happy ...um ...b-birthday ..." I was so surprised that *I* almost fell off the kid-sized chair. Jimmy Spoon pointed to the opposite chair and said,

"Do you ... um ... mind ... if ... if I..." I nodded and he sat down. "Have you ... um ... had ...had ... a nice ...uh ... day?" he asked.

"It's been okay," I said.

"I'm ...um ... sorry your ... um ... family ...uh ... couldn't ..." he trailed off. "B-babs ... um ... emailed me ..."

"Oh," I said. I was still too surprised to say much but I was already getting used to his twitches and stammer. He pulled something out of his rucksack and handed it to me. It was a thin book in a yellow cover. On it, it said "POEMS by James Spoon". He reached over and opened the cover. Inside, he'd written "Vicky - have a good day. James Spoon" . I flicked through it. It was only about twenty pages with two short poems to a page but I got this nice warm glow and found myself smiling at him.

"Thanks Jimmy!" I said. "I didn't think you'd had anything published!"

"Oh ... um ... I got that ...um ...printed privately a

31

few … um …years ago and … I give - gave them to people I … um … know …"

I didn't know what to say but then heard myself ask him,

"Do you like pizza?"

10 - My Fan Club Stuff

It's Friday. Last night, me Nana and Jimmy Spoon went for dinner at Pizza Parlour. I wore my new dress and everything and Nana wore her black jeans and the white top with the gold flower on it. Jimmy Spoon *wasn't* wearing odd trainers for a change. Instead he had on some nice black shoes - very shiny. I still don't know why he wears odd trainers sometimes. I shall have to ask him.

At the restaurant we had the best time. The waiters had put three balloons over the table which was a nice surprise, and some party poppers by our plates. Nana and Jimmy Spoon talked a lot - and Nana is quite right about him losing his stutter whenever he talks about his writing. I didn't mind them talking. I think they must have been good mates at Nana's writing class. I liked listening and they made it sound like loads of fun so I wondered if there was a Creative Writing class *I* can go to. I said to Nana,

"Does anyone do writing courses for kids?"

"Well I don't know," said Nana. "Maybe we can have a look on the internet? Or ask Bev. Why do you want to know?"

"It just sound really cool," I said. "I'd go to one if there was one near us..." Nana looked at me a bit oddly then said,

"Okay, we'll look into it. Now eat your pizza before it gets cold."

After a bit, I started feeling tired. After all I *had* been at school all day. Nana must have noticed because all of a sudden, the waiters carried a cake in with eleven candles on it, and everyone there sang Happy Birthday to me - even people we don't know - as I blew the candles out. Then they put the cake into a square white box and Nana ordered a cab home for us. On the way home, I said,

"I like Jimmy Spoon, Nana. Was he your boyfriend?"

"Boyfriend?" Nana laughed. "Whatever makes you think that?"

"I dunno," I shrugged. "You just seem to be really good mates and I was just wondering."

"Well you can stop wondering," said Nana. "Jimmy Spoon has never been my boyfriend. He's far too young for me. We just got on very well all through the course. Then he moved to Jersey and we lost touch. And now we've met up again, we've just got a lot of catching up to do."

"So why did he move to Jersey?" I asked.

"He was working there. He lived in St Helier," said Nana.

"Would you *like* him to be your boyfriend?" I asked.

"What's all this about boyfriends?" Nana asked.

"If you get one what will happen to me?" I said.

"Nothing will happen to you, Popsicle, because I'll never get one. I am much too busy - and happy - looking after you."

When we got home, Nana put the cake into the kitchen and I went straight upstairs to get ready for bed. She came up and said goodnight and I slept really well - which surprised me because I haven't been sleeping much since Mum rang to say they wouldn't be home. And then this morning, the postman brought a letter for me. It's from the Dickie Doyle Fan Club. I couldn't wait to open it and see his autographed photo and I ripped it open. Even Nana got excited. When I opened the envelope, all these bits and pieces fell onto the table cloth. There was a Wizardatron badge, a Dickie Doyle Key Fob, a Dickie Doyle notebook and pen, a fan club badge, a newsletter and - last of all - a postcard which landed face down. Me and Nana looked at each other. At last we'd see what Dickie Doyle looks like.

"Go on," said Nana. "Turn it over." I closed my eyes for a second. I had this picture in my head. Dickie Doyle would be tall and blond with blue eyes, and he'd be wearing a blue shirt - I just knew it. His writing always *sounds* like he looks like that.

"Turn it over," said Nana again. So I did. And it wasn't a photograph at all! It showed the front cover of the first Wizardatron book - and across it was scribbled the words 'All The Best - Dickie Doyle'. What a let-down! I couldn't believe it - and I don't think Nana could either.

"What a pity," she said. She held the card right up to her face. "At least it does look like he's actually signed it and it isn't printed. Just think, Vicky. He might have signed this card with the very same pen he writes his books with …"

"But is isn't a photograph!" I said. I was really disappointed and I didn't think it was fair. "How's anyone going to know who he is? It might as well be Jimmy Spoon touring!"

"Never mind," said Nana. "Don't be too disappointed. You can stick these in your scrap book before you go to school. There's plenty of time." She lifted the newsletter and flicked through it.

"Oh look," she said. "On the back there's a list of the book shops he's going to visit during the tour …" She stopped suddenly and stared. Then she looked over at me.

"What?" I asked.

"The first shop on the tour," she said. "It's Benjy's …"

"What?" I screeched. She gave the sheets to me and I stared in amazement. It really did say Benjy's - *our* Benjy's. It was as clear as anything. He'll be there on 16th July. That's only four weeks away. I forgot about being disappointed and I started cheering. Nana got straight on the phone and talked to Benjy.

"What fantastic news, Benj!" she said. "Yes - about Dickie Doyle. Really? And you weren't allowed to say anything till the newsletters went out. Amazing. How long have you known? You're kidding me. Well you kept that very quiet, didn't you." They chatted for a few more minutes then Nana said,

"Would you really? Brilliant! No. Not a word till you confirm. Thanks, Benj."

"Confirm what?" I asked.

"The time," she answered. "She's going to come back to me." She glanced at the clock.

"Better get a move on if you want to stick these in your scrapbook before school …"

Everyone at school seemed to know about Benjy's. I didn't know so many of them were Dickie Doyle fans. It was all anyone would talk about. The head teacher even announced it during assembly. And then - during English - Miss Rupert said there was going to be a poetry contest to celebrate the tour. She's running the competition until the week before the end of term and the winning poem will be published in the local paper and put on show at the library. There'll also be a £50 book voucher.

"So," she said. "Who'd like to enter?"

"Vicky will," said Jennifer Armstrong. "She's always got her nose in a book …"

"There is nothing wrong with having one's nose in a book, Miss Armstrong," Miss Rupert said. She looked at me. "Would you like to enter, Miss Price?"

36

"No, Miss," I said. "I'm going to be a *writer* not a poet …"

"Will you at least think about it?" she wanted to know.

"Maybe," I said. But I know I won't.

11 - My Poem

Nana and Jimmy Spoon keep emailing each other. She keeps saying she's just glad that they're back in touch - but I'm not so sure. I suppose if she gets a boyfriend I should be glad it's someone like Jimmy Spoon. But I still don't know what would happen to me so most of the time I try not to think about it. It is nice they're goods mates though. She worries about me not having friends - and she's a fine one to talk! But ever since he turned up, she just seems to be in a really good mood *all the time*. Not that she often gets in a bad mood - but just lately she's looked like a little kid on Christmas Eve, you know? As if something amazing is about to happen. If they do fancy each other I expect I'll get used to it. She says he's too young for her but my dad's much older than my mum so you never know.

Anyways - when I told Nana about the competition at school, she begged me to go in for it. I said that I want to be a writer like Dickie Doyle not a poet like Wordsworth - but she says lots of people are both - like Roald Dahl - so why not at least give it a go. She could be right. I have written a few stories but I have never tried poetry so, to help me, she has lent me her published stuff to read through. I have also read the little book Jimmy Spoon gave me and you know what? I am starting to quite like poetry after all. I am surprised by that but I suppose I shouldn't be. When you think about it, what's the first thing we learn when we're really little? Nursery Rhymes!

And yesterday, at the library, I found this book of poems that were *all* written by kids. One of them is by a girl who was only five years old   - and she's had it published already! Not one of the poets in that book is over twelve so I thought to myself - well, if *they* can do it, why shouldn't I? So I got the book out and brought it home and me and Nana read through it last night. It's kind of funny because I only ever think of published writers as being grown-ups - and when I said so to Nana we went on the internet to see if we could find out about other kids who have had stuff published. There's quite a lot. The most famous one is Anne Frank. Have you ever heard of her? She was thirteen when she started keeping a diary and then her and her family had to go into hiding in Amsterdam because of the war. It is sad that she didn't live to see the diaries published - but Nana says it is one of the world's greatest ever selling books even after all this time. So I am going to see if there's one at our library and get it out so I can read it. Nana also asked me if I am still keeping my diary so I said that I am, kind of, and showed it to her. She flicked through it and said,

"Hmm - you've done quite a bit haven't you?" I nodded and she suddenly said, "What's this about me and Jimmy Spoon?" I snatched it away.

"Nothing," I said as my face got hot. A funny little smile appeared on her face.

"Can I read it when you've finished it?" she asked.

"No," I said quickly. "Er … maybe …but I don't know when it'll be finished do I? I might never finish it so …you might never get to read it. Ever."

"Popsicle," said Nana. "Jimmy Spoon is not my boyfriend …"

"I never said he was, did I?" I asked. "Anyway I can't show it to you now. I need it. I want to try to write my poem …"

I took it back up to my room and sat at my desk. I am

no good at telling lies to Nana because she always knows so there's no point. And because I told her I wanted to try my poem now, I thought I'd better give it a go. For a long time I sat staring out of the window. Then I made a plan. I thought that if I write the *longest poem ever* then that would mean I've worked harder and I'd be bound to win. So I started it at long last and a bit later, Nana came in to see how I was getting on. I showed it to her. Here's the first few lines.

There was a baby in a nappy.
The baby wasn't very happy.
A bird was flying in the sky.
The bird was flying very high.

Nana read it and said,
"Are you pleased with it?"
"Yes," I said.
"And are you going to finish it?"
"Yes." I said and told her about my plan to write the longest poem ever. She said,
"First of all, a poem does not have to be long to be good."
"Oh," I said.
"I mean it's okay to write a long poem if it has got a bit of a story to it. Or it means something to you that you might want to share with other people."
"Right," I said.
"Secondly," she went on. "A poem doesn't *have* to rhyme - did you know that?"
"No," I said. I thought *all* poems have to rhyme. Isn't that why they're poems? If they're not going to rhyme, doesn't that just make them stories?
"No," said Nana. "A good poem doesn't have to be long and it doesn't have to rhyme. In fact .... hang on a tick ..." She went off and came back with a small book in

40

her hands which she gave to me. The book was called 'A Little Bit Of Haiku'.

"Hike what?" I said.

"Haiku," said Nana. "It is based on a Japanese poetry form. You know about syllables, don't you? Yes - of course you do - silly Nana. Well a haiku is a poem that is just *seventeen* syllables long. That's seventeen *syllables*, not seventeen words. But some people think that haiku are the most profound poems ever written. This book contains some of the best haiku by some of the real masters - Basho, Issa, Buson ..."

I was staring at her in amazement. She was talking really fast and sounded really excited - so excited that she made me want to try writing haiku straight away. I bet she was good at teaching. Especially about words because she just loves them so much. She smiled at me.

"Read these," she said. "And you'll see what I mean ..."

12 - My Very Serious Talk With Jimmy Spoon

I have read all the haiku in Nana's book. At first, I couldn't really make them out, but the more I read and talked to Nana, the more I got it. One thing's for sure. My nana loves her writing. She's been doing more and more of it lately so maybe meeting up with Jimmy Spoon again has been good for both of them? I watch her as she writes and she gets really lost in it and sometimes I have to say something two or three times before she hears me. And I didn't know just how much she's had published so I am feeling really proud of her. The whole writer-thing is so different to what I thought it was. There are really famous writers like Dickie Doyle and Roald Dahl and Enid Blyton who *everyone* has heard of. Then there's really busy ones like Nana and Jimmy Spoon who aren't famous at all. It makes me think sometimes.

After reading 'A Little Bit Of Haiku', I went to the library and asked Bev where I could find some more. I think she was surprised that I knew what they are and she showed me where to find them. I read loads in the library then brought some books of them home. When I got in, Nana had a visitor. It was Jimmy Spoon! So much for him not being her boyfriend.

"What … what's this … um … then?" he asked as I put the books on the table. I showed him.

"Not … uh … Dickie … um … Doyle, then?" he asked. I shook my head. It's funny but since I started reading poems I've hardly even thought about Dickie Doyle. Or Wizardatron.

"I made the mistake," said Nana, "of introducing Vicky

to haiku the other day."

"Haiku excellent," said Jimmy Spoon without a twitch or stammer. I nodded.

"They're really cool," I said, opening one of the books. He turned it round so he could see the page then he said,

Beginning of spring -
the perfect simplicity
of a yellow sky

"That's by a man called Issa," said Nana. I couldn't believe it. Jimmy Spoon read it so well - really clearly and slowly - and I just wanted to hear him read out another, and another and another. He changed when he read them out. Hearing him made me come out in goose bumps and I felt like I held my breath forever. I stared at him because I just couldn't help it. When he realised, he went purple, knocked the book flying and almost spilt his mug of coffee.

"Um ... I ... uh ..." he said. And suddenly, he was just Jimmy Spoon again.

"Wow, Jimmy," I said. "That was good. It was really, really good."

"I ... um ... like reading ...poetry ..." he said. "I like ... poetry ..."

"Have you got a favourite poem?" I asked.

"Oh ... um ... lots ... lots of ... um ... favourites ..." he answered.

"So what's your most favouritest of all then?" I asked.

"'Favouritest'?" laughed Nana. "What kind of word is that?" Honest - Nana and her words. Sometimes she talks like she swallowed a dictionary for breakfast. Jimmy Spoon didn't even flinch. He just thought for a second then said,

"Favouritest would b-be … um … 'If' b-by … um … Rudyard Kipling or mayb-be … um …" He stopped, closed his eyes for a second then said softly,

What is this life if full of care
we have no time to stand and stare?

No time to stand beneath the boughs
and stare as long as sheep and cows.

No time to see when woods we pass
where squirrels hide their nuts in grass.

No time to turn at beauty's glance
and watch her feet how they dance.

No time to wait till her mouth can
enrich the smile her eyes began.

A poor life this if full of care
we have no time to stand and stare.

He said it so well that, for a second, I even felt tears in my eyes. When he finished, the last few words just sort of trailed off, then he opened his eyes and saw us both looking at him. Me because the Jimmy Spoon who talks and the Jimmy Spoon who says poems are like two different Jimmy Spoons. And Nana … well … she was looking at him the way Mum looks at Dan sometimes - like she's bursting with pride.

"That's … um …b- by W H Davies," he said. "It's … um … called … uh …'Leisure'."

Jimmy Spoon stayed to dinner and soon him and Nana were back to talking about the writing classes again. Its sounds like they loved it and I wondered again why there's no writing classes for kids. Not learning-to-do-joined-up-writing but proper story or poem writing classes. There's none round our way anyway. But there's soccer academies and dancing schools and drama classes, music teachers, singing clubs, choirs - everything kids might be interested in *except* writing classes. It doesn't make sense. After dinner, I said to Jimmy Spoon,

"You know what? When you said that poem and read out the haiku, you didn't stammer or anything. Why don't you ask Bev if you can read some at the library?"

"Um ... I did ...uh ... ask b-but I ... think ... my stutter ... put ... put her off ..." he said.

"But that's because she's never heard you read anything, Jimmy," I said.

"I ... need ... need to ..." he said. "B-but ... I get so ... so ..."

"Tongue tied?" I asked. He nodded. "Well if you pretend you're reading a poem every time you need to talk," I went on, "maybe that will help you out?" He looked at me a bit weird for a second then he closed his eyes and said,

"Vicky - you're - a - genius. Thank you. You've ..." he paused, took a deep breath then said, "you've saved my life!" Then he opened his eyes and smiled at me. A proper big smile not his funny little half smile.

Nana and me cheered and cheered. We got him talking for ages after that and he got better and better as he went on.

When he was pulling his jacket on to go, I said to him,

"So, will you go and see Bev again?"

"I'll ... think ...ab-bout it," he said carefully.

"I'll make a deal with you," I said. "You do a reading

and I'll try really, really hard with my poem for the competition." He nodded and we spat on our hands and shook.

"Deal," we both said.

After he'd gone, Nana said,

"I'm so proud of you, Vicky."

"What about?" I asked.

"What you said to Jimmy. It was really clever of you to think of it." She kissed me. "Sometimes, my Popsicle," she said, "you're eleven going on thirty." Eleven going on thirty? What does that mean when it's at home?

13 - My Haiku

For the past couple of days, me and Jimmy Spoon have been meeting at the library straight after school. We find a big cushion and put it into the corner, then we both sit with our backs against the wall. For the first ten minutes, we just read to ourselves. Then I start to write and he chooses a poem to read out. When he's decided which one - yesterday it was 'The Owl And The Pussycat' and today it was one called 'Daffodils' - he reads it to himself a few times then he says,

"Ready when you are ..." Then he reads the poem out. This is the best bit. If you could hear him read you'd know what I mean. It's not just his voice. It isn't even because he doesn't stammer or twitch. It's because he's like the best actor in the world. Like he acts he poem out just with his voice. Nana says it's because he's living the poem as if he's really part of it. It is just so cool to hear him. And the biggest surprise of all is that, for the first few minutes after he's finished, he's so ordinary. Today, I said to him,

"It really works then?"

"What?" he asked.

"Pretending you're reading a poem out whenever you say something," I answered.

"It - is - amazing," he said slowly and clearly. He looked at me. "I -don't - know - how - to - thank you."

"That's okay," I said. For a second he looked like he was going to say something else about it but then he said, instead,

"Right ... um ...your - turn ..."

This is the worst bit. I don't think I am very good at

writing poems.   Mine just seem really rubbishy when I think about all the others I have read lately. Why couldn't Miss Rupert run a story-writing contest instead of a poem one? I'd be all right then. The other day, Nana saw me throwing some of mine away. She went ballistic.

"How will you ever know you've written a good poem," she said as she fished them back out of the bin. "If you don't keep the bad ones to compare them to?" She made me promise to give them all to her from now on so she can look after them. Later I saw her putting them into a brown folder.

Today at the library, I thought I'd try something different so I took a deep breath and read my poem out to Jimmy Spoon.

I will never write
a poem that's good enough
till I try haiku

I'd just said the last word when Jimmy Spoon burst out laughing. I have never heard him laugh like that. It was so loud that the little kid on the next cushion nearly jumped out of her skin and burst out crying.

"Do you mind?" hissed the little kid's mum. "This *is* a library you know!" Jimmy Spoon said sorry then grabbed my hand and pulled me out of the library. That surprised me. The only other person to hold my hand like that is Nana - and maybe Dad when I was really tiny. It felt kind of nice.

Outside, he leaned against the wall and laughed and laughed, holding his belly like it might burst any second. I didn't see what was so funny. In fact I was getting crosser by the minute. I thought the haiku was good. It wasn't meant to make people laugh.

"Oh. Vicky," he gasped wiping his eyes with the cuff of his too-big sweatshirt. "You - have - just - got … got to - enter - that - one - for the - competition. You've - got to."

"Why?" I asked. He looked at me.

"B-because it's … it's …" He closed his eyes, took a breath and said. "Because it is brilliant." He didn't seem to be taking the mickey anymore so I said,

"Really?"

"Yes - really," he answered. "We - cool - with - that?" I thought about it for a second then felt myself smile.

"Yes. We're cool with that," I said.

"Come on," he said. "B-better - get - you home."

A bit later, after he'd gone and Nana and me were sitting down to tea, the phone rang. Nana answered it and her face went as white as a sheet.

"Oh my God!" she said. I didn't like the way her eyes were getting bigger and bigger until they were all I could look at. I suddenly got scared as anything.

"Right," Nana said. "Let us know …" She put the phone down and looked at me.

"Oh, Vicky," she said.

"What … what's happened?" I asked in a voice that didn't sound like mine.

"That was your mum, Sweetheart" she said in a voice that didn't sound like her either.

"There's been a horrible accident …"

14 - My Worst Day Ever (and how it got better)

It's Daniel who's had the accident. He was filming underwater and hit his head, knocking himself out. He almost drowned. Nana told me all this after Mum's call. Then Mum called again. Then Dad rang. In fact the phone's hardly stopped ringing for two days.

My brother's a good swimmer so nobody knows how it happened - whether he misjudged how deep it was or if the water level itself had somehow dropped. There's a big investigation going on and filming's been suspended. Dan's in a coma in some hospital in Detroit and Dad's on his way to join Mum at Daniel's bedside.

The front page news has been all about it. The headlines have been things like WIZARDATRON STAR DANIEL IN CRITICAL CONDITION and CHILD ACTOR DANIEL IN COMA. That's scary stuff when it's about your own brother! One paper had a quote from Dickie Doyle who said *'I'm keeping my fingers crossed he pulls through this.'* One nasty reporter even wrote *'How can we be sure this isn't a hoax of epic proportions - more publicity prior to the launch of the new Wizardatron book and the elusive Mr Doyle's much publicised book tour.'* How can something like this be a hoax?

Of course, the It-must-be-so-cool-to-have-a-famous-brother gang have been ringing me non-stop. Jennifer Armstrong was the first.

"Vicky - how awful! I'm so sorry!"

"He's not dead, Jennifer!" I yelled at her. After another

six calls from various girls at school, I got a bad headache and told Nana I wouldn't talk to another soul. Even Uncle Pete rang. That's what Nana calls a 'rarity'. Jimmy Spoon rang. People we haven't heard from in ages have been ringing. There's reporters outside the front gates. It's been nuts.

"Any news, Mrs Anderson?" they keep shouting.

"Aren't you Barbara Anderson the poet?"

"How's your grandson?"

"How's his sister taken it?"

"Will you be flying out to the States?"

"Is it true the new film's been abandoned?"

This is what I mean about having a famous brother being gross. When something like this happens, there's nothing cool about it at all! Poor Dan. I just want him to get better. I want him to tease me again. I want to talk to him on webcam. I want Mum and Dad to bring him home. If you think I cried a lot when no-one could get back for my birthday, think again. How can one person have so many tears? I've hardly stopped since we heard.

This morning, I looked out of the window and saw Jimmy Spoon pushing his way through the reporters. Every time we look, there seems to be more of them. They're camping on Nana's front lawn! As soon as Jimmy Spoon arrived they swamped him, shouting questions like,

"Are you a family friend?"

"Are you Daniel's agent?"

"Is there any news?"

"Has the boy come out of a coma?"

I bashed against the window and yelled at them.

"Leave him alone! Go away!" But they were making too much noise to hear me. I rushed past Nana and opened the font door, charging out of the house and into the crowd.

"Go away!" I screamed. "We don't want you!"

"Uh … Vicky …" Jimmy Spoon said. He was trying to reach me through a forest of notebooks, pens, cameras, mobile phones and laptops.

"Vicky …" I heard Nana yell and she sounded really scared. They all turned towards her and at that second Jimmy Spoon snatched me up and ran into the house where Nana slammed the door in their horrible faces.

"It's … it's …like …like …a mad ….mad house, B-babs!" said Jimmy Spoon as I ran into Nana's arms.

"Are you okay, Popsicle?" she asked.

"I want them to *go away*," I screamed, hoping they'd hear me.

"Let's go into the kitchen," said Nana.

Nana's kitchen is at the back of the house. No reporters have managed to get in the back garden yet but Nana pulled the blinds down anyway. We sat at the breakfast bar and listened to the racket outside.

"What on earth were you thinking, Jim?" Nana asked after it died down. She started making some coffee.

"I was … worried," Jimmy Spoon replied, twitching and ducking. That made me cry all over again.

"Oh no, Nana," I wailed. "It's back. His stammer's come back!" Nana gave me a hug.

"It's okay," she said. "It's just because he's upset. He'll be fine in a minute." Jimmy Spoon took a deep breath and said carefully,

"I - didn't - realise - things - had - go- so b-bad."

"Tell me about it," grouched Nana. She leaned forward and squeezed his hand. "If I'm honest I don't think we can take much more of it."

"I've - got - a - cottage - in - Arundel," Jimmy Spoon

52

said. "You - can - b-both - go - there - if - you - like. Till … till - this -all -dies - down." Oh he *was* trying hard.

"It'll never die down!" I howled. "Not till Daniel's dead. Then they'll have their bloody story!" It was the first time I ever swore in front of my nana. She slowly turned me to face her and said,

"Your brother is not going to die, Vicky. He'll be all right. But he needs both of us to stay strong for him. Can you do that?" I nodded slowly. She was giving me her trust-me look and I knew she was right.

She finished the coffees for herself and Jimmy and handed me a can of coke out of the fridge. After a bit she turned to Jimmy Spoon and said,

"I think the cottage would be good, Jim. She needs to get away from all this and frankly, so do I. Not sure how we'll get out without being mobbed though …"

"I'll - sort -it," said Jimmy Spoon. "You - go - and - pack."

As he made a phone call, Nana and me put a few things into an overnight bag. It felt weird to think we'd be leaving the house but we had to. At least till Daniel's on the mend.

About an hour later, a police car pulled up outside and two big policemen got out. One pushed the reporters back and the other knocked on the door. As we went towards the police car, the questions began again.

"Have there been any developments?"

"Are you flying out to the States today?"

"What's your take on the curse rumour?" Curse rumour? What's that all about? We got into the police car and a minute or two later we were pulling away. Those reporters wouldn't give up though. They were pressing against the windows, running to keep up. I hid my face in Nana's jacket as she kept an arm round my shoulders. After a bit though we lost them and before we knew it, we were at the train station.

"I - owe - you - one, Jack," grinned Jimmy Spoon as we got out.

"Yes you do," laughed the driver. "I'm not a cabbie you know." They wished us the best of luck and drove away so we went to get our train tickets to Arundel As we left the station, Nana said,

"What was that about a curse, Jim?"

"Search - me," said Jimmy Spoon with a shrug. "Seems someone's - said - the Wizardatron film's b-been hexed."

"What by?" I asked. "A real wizard?" It wasn't meant to be a joke but they both laughed so I did too. It felt a lot better than crying.

A couple of hours later, we reached Jimmy Spoon's cottage. It is really tiny and just down the road from Arundel Castle. Downstairs there's a kitchen and living room and upstairs there's a bedroom and bathroom - and that's all there is. There's two beds so I put my stuff on the one nearest the window and Nana put hers on the one nearest the door. Downstairs, Jimmy Spoon was waiting in the titchy kitchen.

"There's a ..." He took a deep breath then carried on, "there's a - shop - just - down - the - road - where - you can b-buy - b-bread and - milk. " He opened the two cupboards on the wall. "Lots of - uh - tinned stuff in here plus - um - tea and - uh - coffee." He opened another cupboard.

"Plates and - stuff - here. Cutlery in the - uh - drawer. Fridge. Cleaning stuff - under - the - sink." He walked into the living room and we followed him. It wasn't big. There was an armchair, a little sofa, a table and two chairs.

"No - uh - TV," he said. "Sorry. I - write - here. Don't - need - any - distractions. There is - uh - a -radio on the - shelf." He looked at me. "Lots of - b-books to - read." He showed Nana how to use the cooker and where the boiler is and the candles 'just in case'.

"Um - games - under - the coffee tab-ble," he said, opening his arms. "That's it, I'm - afraid ..."

"Thanks, Jim," said Nana. "Not sure how we'll ever repay you for all your help though."

"There's - no - phone," Jimmy Spoon said.

"I've got my mobile," said Nana. "I've sent Penelope a text to let them know where we are." Jimmy Spoon handed Nana the keys.

"I've got - to - go. I'll b-be ... b-back tomorrow..."

We waved goodbye from the front door then had another look around the cottage. In the little chest of drawers between our beds, we found some writing magazines and more books. And out the back there was a tiny garden with long grass and two garden chairs.

After our tour of the house, Nana did some soup for us, then we went for a walk.

"I'm glad there's no reporters here, Nana," I said as we followed the big castle walls round towards the little town centre.

"That's what happens when you're very famous sometimes," Nana said. "It isn't always nice, is it?"

We found the shop and Nana bought a few things like bread and milk, breakfast cereal and eggs then we went back to the cottage and put it all away. We'd only been in a few minutes when Nana's mobile rang. She handed it to me. It was Dad.

"Hello, darling," he said.

"How's Daniel, Dad?" I asked in that scared little voice.

"Much better," he answered. "He came out of the

coma an hour ago. He's still groggy and he can't remember a thing. But he's going to be all right." I felt a big grin cross my face I was so relieved.

"I *knew* he would be!" I said. "Are you and Mum okay?"

"We're fine," he said. "So now you can stop worrying. Put Nana back on would you?" They only talked for a few more minutes and, as soon as Nana put down the phone, we hugged and danced like complete idiots.

"I told you he'd be okay, didn't I?" said Nana. "Haven't I always said Nanas Know Everything!"

15 - My Amazing Discovery

It was so great to talk to Dad. Especially now Daniel's getting better. They have promised a web-cam chat as soon as he's well enough. It's funny really. Most of the time, I don't feel like part of this family and I get really fed up with that sometimes. But when something like this happens, we all get really close again. Nana says families are complicated and she's right there.

After the phone call, I decided to have another look at the books and games in the living room.

"Look, Nana," I said. "Monopoly. Scrabble. Maybe we can have a game later?"

"Why not?" said Nana. "There's nothing on the television is there ..." I started reminding her that Jimmy Spoon doesn't have a television then I realised she was teasing and we both laughed. She turned the little radio on and fiddled with it till she found a station she likes.

"Where does Jimmy Spoon live when he's not here, d'you think?" I asked.

"I believe he's got a little flat in town," answered Nana. I have never heard of someone ordinary like Jimmy Spoon having two homes - only film stars and footballers and lottery winners. But Jimmy Spoon never talks about a job so I'm starting to think he must be quite rich somehow, even though he doesn't seem to be. He wears odd trainers after all. Nana says he's a bit eccentric but when I did ask him why, he didn't answer, he just smiled. So he is a bit strange sometimes, there's no doubt about that. I went over to the bookcase - and suddenly couldn't believe what I was seeing.

"Wow!" I gasped. "Look at this, Nana." It was Dickie

Doyle books. Loads and loads and loads of them. Not just one copy of each one either but *lots* of copies. Jimmy Spoon's got more Dickie Doyle books than me!

"I didn't know he's a Dickie Doyle fan!" I said, still amazed. "He's never said anything and he *knows* he's my most favourite writer ever ever *ever!* I pulled one off the shelf, opened it - and nearly fell over. It was signed.

"Look at *this,* Nana," I said. "It says 'Dickie Doyle 2009 '." It was *exactly* like my autographed postcard at home. It even had the smiley face in the '0' of 'Doyle'.

"Well I never," said Nana. She pulled out another book 'Wizardatron 1 - Lost In The Void'. *That* was signed. So I pulled out the next one - 'Wizardatron 2 - Beyond The Universe'. And *that* was signed. In fact we pulled all the books out and *every single one of them was signed by Dickie Doyle!* I don't get it. How comes he has never ever told me about this? Nana was staring at one signature after another and said,

"These must be worth a fortune!"

"Do you suppose he *knows* Dickie Doyle?" I asked. She shook her head.

"I have no idea," she said. "Well," she added. "Let's put these all back. You can ask him tomorrow, can't you." We put them all back on the shelves and I curled up in the armchair with one.

"That's you sorted then," said Nana as she sat at the table. "I don't suppose Scrabble will get a look in now!"

After a bit I looked up and she was writing. I don't actually see her write that often so I asked her what she was doing.

"I've had this idea," she told me.

"For a new poem?" I asked. She shook her head. "Tell me about it then," I said.

"Well, I'm not too sure yet if it will come to anything,"

58

she said. "But do you remember that night at the pizza place when you said about Writing classes for children?" I nodded.

"I think you might be onto something," she said.

"Are you going to start some?" I asked. "Can I come if you do?"

"Not sure yet," Nana said, shaking her head. "I'll need to do some research first."

Later on we went to a Chinese restaurant for dinner. I love egg foo yung so that's what I had and Nana had rice, noodles and some sweet and sour chicken. It was really nice and filled us both up so afterwards, we took a slow walk back to Jimmy Spoon's cottage. It was ten o' clock by the time we got in. It just felt like it had been the longest day so I went straight up to bed. Nana brought me up a glass of milk and sat on her bed so we could chat as I drank it.

"You should sleep better now you know Daniel's going to be all right," Nana said.

"So will you," I said as I snuggled down. She kissed me.

"Sweet dreams," she said. And that's all I can remember.

16 - My Poems

When I woke up this morning, I wanted to write something. That's the first time that's *ever* happened. I want to *be* a writer - and one day I will be. But that's the only time I have wanted to just sit down and *write*. Not sure if that's because Dan's getting better, or because Arundel is *that* kind of place - or if it's just because we're away from the reporters. Or maybe a mix of them all?

It was really early when I opened my eyes. At first, I couldn't even remember where I was. But then I rolled over and spotted Nana asleep in the other bed. She had her mouth open and was snoring a bit, so I knew she wouldn't wake up for a while. I got out of bed and pulled on my dressing gown and slippers before creeping out and very quietly closing the bedroom door. I went to the loo then crept down the steep stairs. I couldn't wait to see all those Dickie Doyle books lined up on Jimmy Spoon's bookcase again. I am going to ask him if I can buy one of each signed copy with my birthday money, only I haven't told Nana that yet.

In the living room, I opened the curtains and then I looked at the books. I still couldn't believe he had so many of them - four copies of Wizardatron 1, five of Wizardatron 2 and at least three or four of all the others. Mostly I couldn't believe he'd never said anything. I mean that's weird. Anyway, as I flicked through a couple of them, I decided to text Jimmy Spoon and ask him about them. I know his number's on Nana's mobile (I still think he's her secret boyfriend but she won't admit it) so I thought I'd do it straight away. Then I remembered - Nana's mobile was upstairs. She must have taken it up last night in case anyone rang with news of Daniel. And I haven't got a mobile of my own yet. That's something else I might get with my birthday money after we get home. After a bit, I sat at the little table and looked out of the window. It was *really* quiet. So different to where we live. And *that* was when I got the idea for a new poem.

I hunted about for some paper and a pen, and when I found some, I began to write. This isn't for Miss Rupert's poetry competition though. It's to send to Daniel. I'll copy it into a get well soon card and send it later - if Nana's got the address anyway. Or can get it. When it was finished I was pleased with it. I think it might even be the best thing I've written so far and that's really cool. I think it's good because I *wanted* it to be good because I love Daniel and I'm proud of him. And if he ever finds out I said that and puts it all over Facebook, I won't mind a bit. And then I got a big surprise because I wrote *another* poem straight after. That one was about Nana. And I was just finishing a *third* one when Nana got up and came down. It was half past eight and I'd been writing for two hours. But it went by so quickly it didn't *feel* like two hours.

"Why didn't you come and wake me?" Nana asked with a big yawn.

"I didn't want to," I said. "It's not like we've got anything special to do today, is it?"

"I suppose not," said Nana, pulling cornflakes out of the cupboard. "There you go again Miss-Eleven-Going-On-Thirty."

"What do you mean by that?" I asked. "You keep saying it but I don't know what you mean." She kissed my head.

"It means that sometimes you sound too grown up to only be eleven," she said. "Now give me a hand with breakfast, there's a good girl." I got the orange juice out of the fridge and put it onto the little table with two beakers.

"What've you been doing anyway?" Nana asked.

"Writing," I answered.

"Writing what?" Nana wanted to know. "Your diary?"

"No. Poems," I replied.

"Oooh, let me see," she said. We sat down to eat and I pushed the poems towards her. As she munched, I watched her read then she said with a smile,

"This one about Daniel is lovely, Popsicle."

"I'm going to send it to him," I told her. "Have you got the address of the hospital?"

"Let's wait and find out when he's coming home first, shall we?" she said. She read the next poem - the one about her.

"Oh, Vicky," she said afterwards. "What lovely words. Thank you, darling. Will you copy it out for me?"

"If you want," I said. Then she read the third poem.

"Is this one for the competition?" she asked. I nodded. She smiled and passed them back.

"Well done," she said. "I knew you could do it if you put your mind to it." I was pleased she said that and I smiled.

After breakfast, I went upstairs for a bath and Nana came up a bit later to wash my hair.

"Will I get into trouble for missing school again, Nana?" I asked as she squidged lather through my hair.

"Stop worrying. I've spoken to them. Apart from the other week, you haven't even had any time off sick in over a year." She began to rinse my hair with a jug full of water. "It's not as if you're off every other day."

"Nana," I said. "Is Daniel really going to be okay?"

"Of course he is," she answered. She squeezed all

the water out of my hair then rubbed it with a towel. "Now - out you get. And you can go and dry off while I have my bath. Then we'll decide what to do for the day. Jimmy texted me last night. He thinks he'll be here around three and he wants to take us out for dinner. So we've got the whole morning to fill."

I dried myself in the bedroom then got dressed. While I waited downstairs for Nana, I wrote this letter -

Dear Dickie Doyle.

My name is Victoria Price and my brother is Daniel Price who is in the Wizardatron film. I am writing to ask you if you know my friend Jimmy Spoon? He is a writer like you. I sent you a letter a long time ago but you didn't answer it. I want to know what time you'll be at Benjy's on 16th July because Benjy is my Nana's friend and her book shop is just down the road from our house. I want to show you a poem I have written and ask you to help me be a writer like you and Jimmy Spoon and my nana who is a poet called Barbara Anderson. Do you know her? I am going to send this letter to your fan club and I hope you get it before the tour starts. I joined your fan club. Thank you for the autograph. Your Number One Fan, Victoria Price, age 11.

I will post it when I get home. I hope he answers it.

17 - My Discovery About Jimmy Spoon

I am sitting at the little table by the window. Nana is doing scrambled eggs on toast for our lunch. My diary is getting a bit full now. I might have to buy another one with my birthday money. I won't have any birthday money left, soon, will I?

After lunch, Nana and me are going to a Wildfowl Trust place which isn't far from here. She has got a thing about birds, my nana. She keeps a list of all the different ones she's seen and she's seen millions of them. There's meant to be all kinds of different ones at this place and Nana keeps moaning because she forgot her camera when we left home and can't take any pictures. Anyways after breakfast, we found this leaflet about this place and decided to give it a go. We didn't go earlier because it was raining but it looks like it's stopped now. And I'd better stop too because here comes lunch. Back later.

****

Hello again. We just got back from our walk. I bought a notebook and pen at the Wildfowl place. It was all right. I got a bit bored with it. All I could hear was Nana going "Oooh!" and "Ahhh!" It was a bit embarrassing. And now we have come back to Jimmy Spoon's cottage and he will be here soon so we are getting ready to go out for dinner. Nana's all excited again. I don't care what she says, he is definitely her secret boyfriend. If I ever see them kissing though I think I will throw up! Nana asked me why I bought the notebook. It is a really nice one with pink flamingos on the front cover. I told her it was because my diary is nearly full up so of course all she kept asking then was when could she read it? So then I told her I want to write a story in it instead. Now I know I can write poems, I want to try writing a brand new story.

Earlier on, we found some interesting books on Jimmy Spoon's bookcase. Apart from all the Dickie Doyle ones I mean. One is called "The Writer's And Artist's Year Book" and the other one is called "The Writer's Handbook". Nana says they are 'essential tools' for the writer because they have got lists in of all the publishers and editors a writer might need. She said she's got a couple at home herself - plus one called "The Poet's Handbook" - and *she* says she'd be lost without them. She told me that when she was a kid, she used to go to the local library and sit on the floor and copy the names out because she didn't have enough money to buy one of her own. So as well as my mobile phone and my new diary and all the signed Dickie Doyle books I'm going to get with my birthday money, I also want to get one of these writer's books just to prove to everyone how serious I am about wanting to be a writer. It will be worth it when I'm famous like Dickie Doyle.

Dad rang again a little while ago. Daniel should be okay to fly home on the same day Dickie Doyle starts his book tour. The doctors have said he needs a month of complete rest. So in two weeks time, they'll all be home again and I can't wait. And I'll get to meet Dickie Doyle at Benjy's, I just know it. I like it when things work out. And I know Daniel's getting better because there's only half a page about him in today's "Daily Mail". The front page has been taken over by news of a lady in Somerset who had *six* babies all in one go! My guess is that this means the reporters will be gone and we can go home. It's nice at Jimmy Spoon's cottage and Arundel is pretty. But it isn't home. And I need to get back to school and hand my poem in.

****

Jimmy Spoon has just arrived. I went straight up to him and said,

"Do you know Dickie Doyle? I saw all the signed books. Is he a friend of yours?" Nana said,

"Vicky, don't be so rude … sorry, Jim, she's got this bee in her bonnet …"

"But do you?" I asked. Jimmy Spoon looked a bit surprised. He went red and said,

"Um…"

"Tell me," I said. "Do you know him?" Jimmy Spoon looked at Nana then *he* surprised *me.* when he said,

"Yeah … kind of …"

18 - My First Grown Up Chat With Nana

I knew it! I knew it! I just knew it! And now *you* know that *I* know *somebody* who *really knows* Dickie Doyle - my most favourite writer ever ever *ever*! At first I clapped and cheered and stamped my feet and I *so* wanted to say to Jimmy Spoon how much I want to meet Dickie Doyle and ask him how he got to be a great author and where does he get his ideas and please, please, *please* could I have his autograph and ask him to help me to be a great author too ... but then I realised I'd sound just like those idiot girls at school who think that having a famous brother is sooo cool and *please* could I get Daniel's autograph for *them* ... and that stopped me in my tracks.

The more I thought about it the more sense it made really. Nobody in the world can have that many signed books and *not* know the writer - especially one like Dickie Doyle who's never done a tour before - how else would Jimmy Spoon have got them?

"Why didn't you tell me?" I asked. Jimmy Spoon shrugged his shoulders.

"I - don't - know - him - that - well ..." he said slowly as he went purple with embarrassment. I felt my heart hit the pit of my stomach. What did he mean by 'that well'? And there was me thinking they were real old mates who met up for a drink sometimes or went to play golf - or whatever it is grown-up men do.

"We - were at - the- same - school - kind of ..." said Jimmy Spoon.

"What do you mean 'kind of', Jimmy? " I asked. I was starting to feel cross - and that was the first time I'd *ever* been cross with Jimmy Spoon. I mean what's the big deal here? He either knows Dickie Doyle or he doesn't - why not just give me a straight answer?

I must have opened my mouth to speak again but I saw Nana looking at me and shaking her head.

"That's enough for now, Vicky," she said. "I'm sure Jim's got his reasons. He'll tell us when he's ready - if there's anything *to* tell - isn't that right?" She looked at Jimmy Spoon who was so purple now that I thought he'd pop like a balloon. He shrugged again and gave a half nod.

I don't know about you but I felt there was something a bit strange about all this. For a start, the websites say Dickie Doyle's in his mid-30s and we all know Jimmy Spoon's much younger than that so they *couldn't have been* at school together could they? And even if they were - why would Jimmy Spoon have so many signed books if he only knew him 'kind of'? There's something someone's not telling me - but what?

"I'm not stupid you know," I muttered.

"Nobody said you're stupid, Vicky," said Nana crossly. "Now stop being silly. We're going out for dinner and tomorrow we can go home. Let's try to enjoy the evening shall we?" She looked at Jimmy Spoon who shook his head and said,

"She's - had - a rough - week. It's okay."

Nana looked back at me so I said,

"Sorry, Jimmy. I didn't mean to be nosy." He smiled then said.

"Nothing - to - b-be - sorry ab-bout!"

A bit later we set off for dinner. Jimmy Spoon wanted us to try this posh burger place. When we were sitting down and eating, we told Jimmy Spoon the great news about Daniel.

"Mayb-be," he began, "you should - have - joint -

party? Late - b-birthday for - Vicky and - uh - welcome home for - Daniel?"

"Great idea," said Nana. "What do you think Popsicle?" I nodded - my mouth full of French Fries.

"Oh - and have you told Jimmy about your poems?" said Nana.

"Poems?" Jimmy Spoon asked.

"She wrote three this morning," said Nana sounding proud. "Really good ones, too. Why don't you show Jimmy when we get back, Vicky?"

"Are - they - for - the -um - uh competition?" Jimmy Spoon wanted to know.

"One is," I said.

"Well done!" Jimmy Spoon said lifting his glass. "A - toast to - B-babs, Daniel and - Vicky ..." We all clinked glasses but I still didn't feel right. Do you know how it feels when someone's keeping secrets from you? That's how I felt. And it was getting worse and worse. I was finding it hard to swallow. If that's how it feels to start growing up you can forget it. It isn't comfy.

When we got back to the cottage, I went straight upstairs to get ready for bed and a few minutes later, Nana brought me a glass of milk.

"Are you all right, Popsicle?" she asked, ruffling my hair. "You haven't been yourself all evening. I leaned back against the pillows and said,

"Nana, when you were my age - did you always know when grown-ups told you lies?" Nana looked away for a second.

"Who ... who's been lying to you?" she asked.

"Jimmy Spoon," I answered, looking at her carefully. "And you." I was used to seeing Jimmy Spoon blush - he does it all the time. I'd never seen Nana blush before though but she did then.

"Me?" she asked. "Why would I lie to you, darling?"

"Because I'm a kid," I said. She looked at me.

"What do you think I've been lying about?" she asked.

"I think you knew Jimmy Spoon knows Dickie Doyle," I said. "I think you've known for ages. It's not fair, Nana. Grown-ups are always telling kids not to tell lies but grown-ups lie all the time. Mum and Dad both said they'd be home for my birthday. They promised. Then they weren't. That was lying."

"That wasn't lying, Vicky," said Nana. "Circumstances changed. They couldn't have known they wouldn't get back."

"Then they shouldn't of promised," I said.

"But they'll all be home soon, won't they?" she said.

"As long as the *circumstances* don't change again ..." I said. In all the time I've lived with Nana I have never known her not to have an answer - but she looked like she was struggling this time.

"Oh, Vicky, " she sighed. She leaned forward and hugged me. But for once I didn't hug her back. I didn't feel like it.

"Ahem..." said Jimmy Spoon from the door. "Er - can I - um - come in?" Nana looked at me and I nodded. He cleared his throat again then said

"I'm - uh - sorry, Vicky."

"Sorry?" I asked. He nodded.

"I - haven't - b-been - honest with you -" (as if I didn't know!) "- and I - think - think you're - right ..." He looked at me. "I do - know - Dickie - Doyle - properly." He sat on Nana's bed and said,

"B-babs - I think she has - the - right - to - know ..."

"Know what?" I asked.

"Um - everything ..." said Jimmy Spoon.

And that's when he told me.

70

19 - My Unbelievable Two Weeks

It's been a couple of weeks since I wrote but when I tell you why, you'll understand. That night, Jimmy Spoon *did* tell me everything. In fact, he talked for over an hour with hardly any stammering and no twitches at all. And the more he said, the more amazed I got. Everything started to make perfect sense and I couldn't understand how I hadn't realised sooner. There was enough clues and enough coincidences - but I just didn't get it. I mean how thick am I?

Afterwards, when he and Nana had gone back downstairs, I didn't think I'd sleep but I slept really well and the next day, Sunday, Nana and me got the train home. I think she could see how shocked I still was because she kept asking me if I was okay. All I kept saying, over and over again, was "I can't believe it!" Because I *couldn't* believe it. Have you guessed yet what Jimmy Spoon told me? Keep thinking about it. See if you get it quicker than I did. I'll tell you in a bit if you still haven't.

On Monday, I went back to school and handed my poem and my haiku into Miss Rupert. Quite a few kids entered the competition in the end. It's nice to think one of mine might win but I can't see it. And if they don't, it won't really matter. It *is* my first competition after all, and - as Nana said - it's good practice whatever happens. At least I went in for it so I've kept my half of the deal. Jimmy Spoon has kept his as well - just not the way I thought he would as you'll see soon enough.

I spoke to Daniel on web-cam a couple of days later. He looked a lot better than I thought he would and he said he can't wait to get home again for a couple of weeks. Then I got a real surprise because I spoke to Mum and Dad as well. They were using Dad's laptop from a hotel room and they looked so happy that I wished I was with them all so I could give them all the biggest, uncoolest hugs ever. Dad said,

"We've missed you so much, Vicky and we can't wait to see you." Mum said,

"Dan's accident meant we've had time to work a few things out and we know how unfair we've been to you. So we've talked it all through and we've got a surprise for you. Tell her, Harrison." Dad reappeared and said,

"We thought we'd make it up to you so we've booked a holiday for all of us. Dan's got to rest up for a bit so they've rescheduled the filming and they're doing all the scenes he isn't in while he has this break, then they'll finish it when he's back with them after the holiday."

"Where are we going?" I asked. Daniel reappeared.

"Disney World in Florida!" he screeched and I screeched too.

"We'll be home in a few days," said Dad squeezing in behind Daniel. "Once you've broken up from school, we'll all fly out together and have the best holiday ever!" Nana squeezed in behind me.

"Nothing can go wrong this time, can it, Harrison?" she asked sounding a bit worried.

"No chance, Babs," Dad replied. "Everything's booked so there's no going back!" I was cheering and Daniel was cheering. I don't think I've ever been so happy. Anyways, we chatted a bit for a few minutes then we all said goodbye. I couldn't believe my good luck! They're all coming home, the film's going to be finished, Daniel's all right, we're all going on holiday together and on 16th July, Dickie Doyle starts his tour. How perfect can things be? And here's another thing.

When we got back from Arundel, Benjy rang Nana with some awesome news. *She's arranged for me to help Dickie Doyle at the signing.* Can you believe it? Here's how it will work. Nana and me will get to Benjy's Books before it opens. Benjy's going to get some scarlet ribbon to tie across the door. Just inside the shop, there'll be a table set up with a scarlet cloth on it and a chair for Dickie Doyle behind it. Benjy and me will arrange a display of Dickie Doyle books on the table and behind the table there'll be a huge poster with the words BENJY'S BOOKS WELCOMES DICKIE DOYLE on it. When it's time for the shop to open, Benjy will make a speech and then introduce me and I'll cut the scarlet ribbon to let everybody in. And we know loads of people will be there because two big adverts and an article have already appeared in the local paper and all the kids at school have said they're going to come. At ten o'clock, Dickie Doyle will come in, then it will be my job to pass him the books to sign. How cool is that?

When the it-must-be-so-cool-to-have-a-famous-brother gang heard about this, something amazing happened! Suddenly everyone wanted to be my friend. It's almost like they respect me more - and it's not just because of my famous brother either! This will take a bit of getting used to, I can tell you. So the whole Dickie Doyle thing has changed everything. Plus - get this - *Jennifer Armstrong even invited me to go bowling with her on her birthday.* That was two days ago and I had the best time. I got two strikes! Everyone clapped and cheered *me* for a change. It was sooo cool. Maybe Nana's right (because let's face it, she's right about practically everything) and I *do* need more mates my own age.

So - have you guessed yet what Jimmy Spoon told

me? Here's a clue. *The library.* Any help? Here's another. *Nana's writing classes.* There yet? One last clue then - and if you still don't get it, I promise I'll tell you. Okay - so the final clue. *Jimmy Spoon's shyness.* Yes? No? Okay here goes …

20 - My Writer

Jimmy Spoon *is* Dickie Doyle! He really, really is. Jimmy Spoon is his real name and Dickie Doyle is his pen-name (Nana calls in a *pseudonym* and Jimmy Spoon calls it a *nom-de-plume* but *pen-name* sounds better to me). That's what Jimmy Spoon and Nana told me that night at the cottage. All this time I've been dreaming of meeting Dickie Doyle - and it turns out I've known him all along! Even now, I can't really believe it. Here's what they said.

Remember those Creative Writing courses my nana used to run for grown-ups? Well, she did them for three years and one day this gangly, pimply, scruff-bag (her words) turned up. He was very shy and barely sixteen and he hardly spoke during the lesson and Nana thought he'd never come back. That was Jimmy Spoon of course. Anyways, on that first night, Nana set the students an exercise which was to write a short story. All the students (Nana says there was about twelve but Jimmy Spoon says it was nearer twenty) went home and wrote their stories and took them back the next time. Nana says Jimmy Spoon's was the best of the lot so she decided to keep an eye on him over the next few weeks. And she was glad she did because his work was always the best - even the other students said so. And whenever it was his turn to read, he did it brilliantly so Nana had a chat with him.

Turned out he'd been writing since he was seven and he'd already had some short stories published. And that was when Nana realised just how talented this odd teenager was. A couple of years after the classes ended, he wrote his first kid's book and says he was gob smacked when it was taken and even more gob smacked when they asked him for some more books. The first Wizardatron one was published when he was twenty-one! It was his idea to use the name Dickie Doyle - and the publishers liked it so it just kind of stuck. Plus it was the publishers who made up about the teaching and family and dog called 'Rex' (derr!) because, *they* said, it made him more kind of like a proper writer - and not a shy guy with a stammer.

One thing Nana never did was keep in touch with her students because, she said, she wanted them to find their own feet and their own style. She kept an eye out for the name 'Jimmy Spoon', though. But of course by then, he was 'Dickie Doyle' and - because he's always said he'd write horror stories like Stephen King - Nana just had no idea that kid's writer Dickie Doyle was her former student! The rest you sort of know - how he was persuaded to do the tour but realised he needed some practice so he went to Bev as Jimmy Spoon because he didn't think she'd believe he was Dickie Doyle - which is pretty much how we got here, really. Nana only found out he was Dickie Doyle when he let it slip in one of his emails - and she couldn't believe it either and he begged her not to tell me because he was worried we'd stop being friends. Like that would ever happen! Apart from Nana he's the best friend I've ever had.

There is a little bit more to tell you and I think it's just as exciting. And it's this - Nana and Jimmy Spoon are going to start a brand new writing academy for children! They're calling it The Anderson Doyle Academy of Creative Writing. It will be for writers under sixteen and it will be held at the library on Saturday mornings. I am its first student! The plan is to get loads of writers and poets and editors and publishers in to do talks and help out kids like me who want to be writers like Dickie Doyle more than anything else in the world. They want to go out to schools and clubs and bookshops too and maybe even go on television. *Anything*, they say, that will make Creative Writing as cool as acting and singing and football and everything else.   Jimmy Spoon says he wishes there'd been classes like that when he was kid because then he would've had more confidence when he got older.

As for me - well Mum, Dad and Dan are due home tomorrow and I can't *wait* to see them, I'm a personal friend of my most favourite writer ever, ever, *ever. Plus* it was *ME* who told Jimmy Spoon to talk like he reads - which *he* says is the most important thing of all. And I believe him. Wouldn't you, if you were me?

Ends

My Poem
by Vicky Price aged 11 years and one month

I like it when the wind blows
and when the hair of my fringe
dances in my eyes.
I like it when it's raining
and the sound it makes as it
pitter-patters on my umbrella.
I like it when it's sunny
and I can feel the warm sun
making my face go red.
And I like it when it's cold and snowy
because then I stay in bed
and read my Dickie Doyles.